The Fat Control

Based on *The Railway Series* by the Rev. W. Awdry

Illustrations by *Robin Davies*

EGMONT

EGMONT

We bring stories to life

First published in Great Britain 2007
This edition published in 2011
by Egmont UK Limited
The Yellow Building, 1 Nicholas Road, London W11 4AN

Thomas the Tank Engine & Friends™

CREATED BY BRITT ALLCROFT

Based on the Railway Series by the Reverend W Awdry
© 2011 Gullane (Thomas) LLC. A HIT Entertainment company.
Thomas the Tank Engine & Friends and Thomas & Friends are trademarks of Gullane (Thomas) Limited.
Thomas the Tank Engine & Friends and Design is Reg. U.S. Pat. & Tm. Off.

HiT entertainment

ISBN 978 1 4052 6971 1
44741/17
Printed in Italy

Stay safe online. Egmont is not responsible for content hosted by third parties.

FSC
MIX
Paper
FSC® C018306

Egmont is passionate about helping to preserve the world's remaining ancient forests.
We only use paper from legal and sustainable forest sources.

This book is made from paper certified by the Forest Stewardship Council® (FSC®),
an organisation dedicated to promoting responsible management of forest resources.
For more information on the FSC, please visit www.fsc.org. To learn more about
Egmont's sustainable paper policy, please visit www.egmont.co.uk/ethical

*T*his is a story about me, Sir Topham Hatt, or The Fat Controller as my engines call me. I have loved trains ever since I was a boy, but engines are sometimes as troublesome as trucks . . .

One morning, The Fat Controller was eating his usual breakfast of toast and marmalade. Lady Hatt was pouring him a cup of coffee, when the telephone rang.

"Bother that telephone!" said The Fat Controller, frowning.

"I'm sorry, my dear," he said to Lady Hatt, a few minutes later. "The engines are not behaving themselves, I must go at once. Engines on my Railway do as they are told!"

When he arrived at the Main Station, there was a tremendous noise. The passengers waiting on the platform were angry.

The Fat Controller went into his office and sat down behind his desk.

Moments later, the Stationmaster knocked on the door. "There's trouble in the shed, Sir," he said. "Henry is sulking. There's no train and the passengers are saying this is a bad Railway."

"Indeed," said The Fat Controller. "We cannot allow that."

At the sheds, The Fat Controller found Gordon, James and Henry looking very cross.

"Come along, Henry. It's time your train was ready," said The Fat Controller, firmly.

"Henry's not going," said Gordon. "We won't shunt like common tank engines. That is Thomas' job."

"We are important tender engines. Fetch our coaches and we will pull them. Tender engines don't shunt!" huffed Henry.

"Oh, indeed," said The Fat Controller. "We'll see about that. Engines on my railway do as they are told."

And he hurried away in his car to find Edward.

"The Yard has never been the same since Thomas left to run his branch line," he thought, sadly. And he took out a handkerchief to mop his brow.

Meanwhile, Edward was shunting.

"Leave those trucks, please, Edward," said The Fat Controller. "I want you to push coaches for me in the Yard."

"Thank you, Sir, that will be a nice change," said Edward, happily.

"That's a good engine, off you go then."

So Edward found coaches for Gordon, James and Henry, and that day the trains ran as usual.

But the next morning, Edward looked unhappy.

Gordon came clanking past, hissing rudely.

"Bless me," said The Fat Controller. "What a noise!"

"They all hiss me, Sir," sighed Edward. "They say tender engines don't shunt and that I have dirty wheels like the trucks. I haven't, have I, Sir?"

"You have nice blue ones, Edward," said The Fat Controller, kindly. "Tender engines do shunt, but we need another tank engine here."

The Fat Controller went to the Workshop and inspected all sorts of engines. At last, he saw a little green tank engine with four wheels.

"That's the one," he thought. The Fat Controller knew a Really Useful Engine when he saw one. "If I choose you, will you work hard?" he said.

"Oh, Sir. Yes, Sir!" peeped the little green engine.

"That's a good engine. I'll call you Percy," smiled The Fat Controller.

And he drove him all the way back to the Yard.

"Edward . . ." he called, "here's Percy. Will you show him what to do?"

Percy soon learned what needed doing, and he and Edward had a happy afternoon.

Then Henry steamed by, hissing as usual.

"Wheeeesh!" little Percy hissed back.

Henry was so surprised, he almost jumped off the track!

The next day, The Fat Controller arrived. Edward, Thomas and Percy were excited.

He told the engines that Henry, Gordon and James were sulking. "They refuse to shunt like 'common tank engines', so I have shut them in the shed. I want you to run the line for a while."

"Common tank engines indeed!" snorted Thomas. "We'll show them."

"And Percy will help, too."

"Thank you, Sir!" whistled Percy, with delight.

Edward and Thomas worked the Main Line, peep-peeping to each other as they passed by.

Percy puffed along the Branch Line, carrying passengers to their stations.

Thomas was worried about Annie and Clarabel, but his Driver and Guard promised to look after them.

There were fewer trains, but the passengers didn't mind. They knew the three naughty engines were being taught a lesson.

In the shed, Gordon, James and Henry were cold, lonely and miserable.

There was no coal for them, no washdown and they missed their passengers.

They wished they hadn't been so silly.

The next morning, The Fat Controller visited the shed. He could see that the engines had learned their lesson.

"We are sorry, Sir," said Gordon.

"We were too big for our buffers!" added James.

"Remember, only Really Useful Engines can work on my railway!" said The Fat Controller. He knew just how to handle difficult engines.

From that moment on, the three tender engines were never rude to tank engines again.